Spud
and the Funny Trees

Illustrations by Pulsar

EGMONT

95% of the paper used in this book is recycled paper, the remaining 5% is an
Egmont grade 5 paper that comes from well managed forests. For more information
about Egmont's paper policy please visit www.egmont.co.uk/ethical publishing

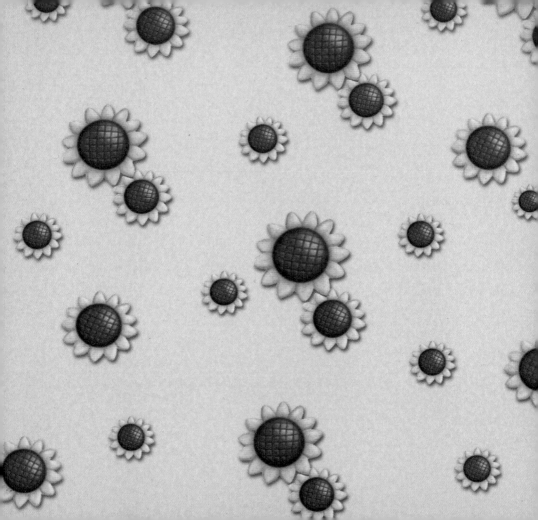

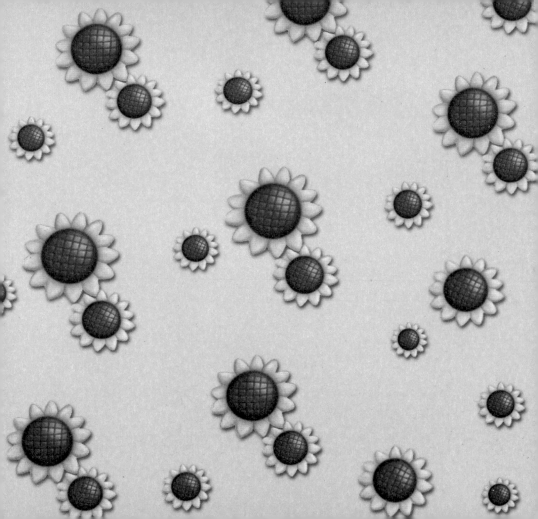

EGMONT

We bring stories to life

First published in Great Britain 2008 by Egmont UK Limited
239 Kensington High Street, London W8 6SA

Based on the television series Bob the Builder © 2008 HIT Entertainment Limited and Keith Chapman.
All rights reserved. The Bob the Builder name and character, related characters and the Bob figure
and riveted logo are trademarks of HIT Entertainment Limited.
Reg. U.S. Pat. & ™. Off. and in the UK and other countries.

HiT entertainment

ISBN 978 1 4052 4109 0

1 3 5 7 9 10 8 6 4 2

Printed in Great Britain

Spud is too noisy and Farmer Pickles has had enough! How can Spud keep quiet and be helpful at the same time?

It was night-time in Sunflower Valley and everybody was in bed. At Scarecrow Cottage, Spud was snoring loudly. Poor Farmer Pickles couldn't sleep!

He sat up in bed, and rubbed his eyes. Then he lay down again wearily and put his pillow over his ears.

Spud's snoring was so loud that Scruffty could hear it too — from his kennel, outside! "Ruff, ruff," whined Scruffty.

At the yard the next morning, Bob told the machines what they were going to do that day.

"We're using these logs to build a safety fence on the riverbank beside Mr Sabatini's windmill," he said.

"A safety fence?" rumbled Roley. "Why?"

Bob laughed. "To stop people from falling into the river, of course!"

Soon, Wendy arrived wearing a lifebelt around her waist. Lofty looked puzzled.

"It's a lifebelt, Lofty," explained Wendy. "You throw it to people if they fall into water and it helps them stay afloat."

"We're going to hang it next to the safety fence," added Bob.

"Well, I'd better be off to the factory," said Wendy, waving goodbye. "I promised to help Farmer Pickles with a big delivery."

At the Sunflower Oil factory, Farmer Pickles was so tired after his noisy night that he arrived very late with his delivery of sunflowers.

"Sorry, I didn't get a wink of sleep last night," he yawned. "Spud is just too noisy! I'm going to have to ask him to move."

Farmer Pickles didn't see that Spud and Scruffty were peeping round the door.

Spud was shocked! "Did you hear that, Scruffty?" he asked. "Farmer Pickles wants me to leave Scarecrow Cottage because I'm too noisy!"

Spud stomped off, crossly. "We'll soon see about that," he said.

As he thudded through the woods, some rabbits hopped across his path.

"Hmm," he wondered. "Rabbits have quiet paws. I wish my feet could be so quiet …"

Spud sat down beside some cork trees. He picked up a piece of bark.

"This is nice and soft," he said to himself. "It must have fallen off this funny tree."

He took a closer look at the tree trunk. "Aha! Spuddie's got an idea!"

Spud began collecting bark from the cork trees. Soon, he had made himself a pair of special cork shoes. "Now I'm as quiet as a rabbit!" he said, tiptoeing on his way.

Meanwhile, on the riverbank, the new safety fence was taking shape.

"Can we build it?" called Bob.
"Yes, we can!" piped the machines.
"Er, yeah, I think so," added Lofty.

They didn't notice Spud creeping up behind them in his new, quiet shoes. Bob had just picked up the lifebelt to hang in its new home, when suddenly Spud tapped him on the shoulder.

"Ta-da!" exclaimed Spud, smiling.

Bob was so surprised that he dropped the lifebelt, which rolled towards Lofty, who was reversing.

"Look out!" cried Bob. But it was too late. Lofty had crushed it.

"Sorry, Bob!" said Spud. "I was just trying to be Silent Spud because Farmer Pickles says I'm too noisy."

Spud showed Bob his quiet shoes.

Bob chuckled. Then he looked more closely at Spud's shoes. "Cork! Of course!" said Bob. He had an idea.

"Let's go and find those cork trees, Muck," he said. "I think they might solve our problem!"

Sure enough, when they reached the wood, Bob found that the bark from the cork trees was light and strong – just right to make a new lifebelt.

Back at the factory, all the bottles of oil were loaded into crates, ready for delivery. There were just enough bottle tops for the bottles.

Travis and Farmer Pickles hadn't gone far when suddenly Spud stepped into their path, still wearing his cork shoes. Travis didn't hear him coming and slammed on his brakes. The crates of bottles in Travis' trailer all crashed and smashed together.

"I'm sorry, Farmer Pickles!" wailed Spud.

Bob was still collecting bark from the cork trees when Wendy telephoned to tell him about the broken bottles. "And there aren't any bottle tops left," she said.

"I might have just the thing – we can use the cork!" said Bob.

Bob and Muck drove straight to the factory. In no time, all the crates of bottles were corked and ready to deliver. "Well done, Spud, for finding the cork trees," said Bob. Spud looked pleased.

Later, Bob hung the new cork lifebelt at the riverbank. The job was finished!

That night, Farmer Pickles told Spud he could stay at Scarecrow Cottage.

"I've made these special earplugs out of cork from your funny trees!" smiled Farmer Pickles. And with that, he put a cork in each ear and fell fast asleep!

Spud was delighted! "Ha-ha! Noisy Spud saved the day!" he laughed.

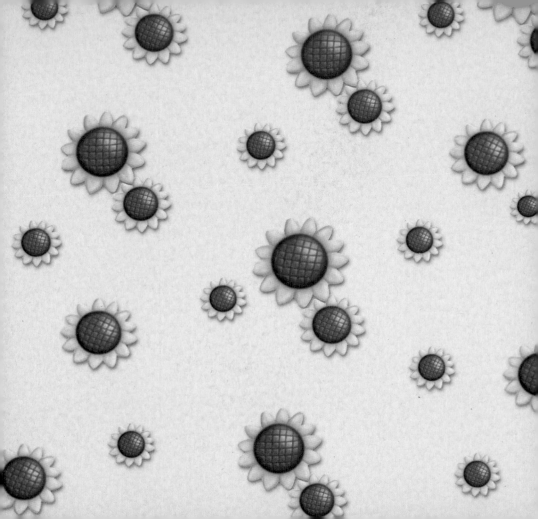

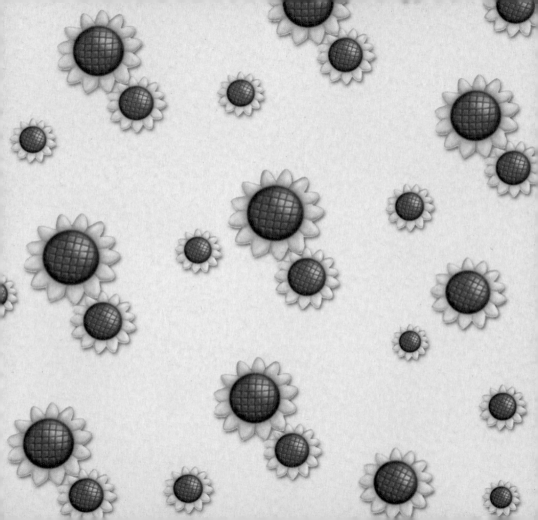

Start collecting your Bob the Builder Story Library NOW!

RRP £2.9

1. Bob and the Big Plan
ISBN: 978 1 4052 3142 8

2. Dizzy and the Talkie-Talkie
ISBN: 978 1 4052 3143 5

3. Scrambler and the Off-road Race
ISBN: 978 1 4052 3144 2

4. Wendy and the Surprise Party
ISBN: 978 1 4052 3140 4

5. Roley and the Woodland Walk
ISBN: 978 1 4052 3750 5

6. Benny and the Important Job
ISBN: 978 1 4052 3748 2

7. Sumsy and the Sunflower Spill
ISBN: 978 1 4052 3747 5

8. Muck and the Machine Convoy
ISBN: 978 1 4052 3749 9

9. Travis and the Tropical Fruit
ISBN: 978 1 4052 4110 6

10. Lofty and the Singing Stars
ISBN: 978 1 4052 4111 3

11. Scoop and the Bakery Build
ISBN: 978 1 4052 4108 3

12. Spud Funny Trees
ISBN: 978 1 4052 4109 0

My Bob the Builder Story Library is THE definitive collection of stories about Bob and the team. Look out for even more terrific titles coming soon!

A fantastic offer for Bob the Builder fans!

NOTE: Style of poster and door hanger may be different from those shown.

In every Bob the Builder Story Library book like this one, you will find a special token. Collect 4 tokens and we will send you a brilliant Bob the Builder poster and a double-sided bedroom door hanger!

Simply tape a £1 coin in the space above and fill out the form overleaf.

EGMONT

www.egmont.co.uk

To apply for this great offer, ask an adult to complete the details below and send this whole page with a £1 coin and 4 tokens, to:

BOB OFFERS, PO BOX 715, HORSHAM RH12 5WG

☐ Please send me a Bob the Builder poster and door hanger. I enclose 4 tokens plus a £1 coin (price includes P&P).

To be completed by an adult

Fan's name:
....

Address:
....

....

Postcode:
....

Email:
....

Date of birth:
....

Name of parent / guardian:
....

Signature of parent / guardian:
....

Ref: BOB 004